Ridin

Written by Patricia Roberts

CONTENTS

Rigby

HOUGHTON MIFFLIN HARCOURT

RIDING THE RIVERS

Rivers can be wild. Riding the rivers in a kayak can be a wild and exhilarating experience. Many rivers have big waves and steep waterfalls. Kayakers need strong boats, special gear, and the skills to keep themselves safe.

Rivers are sometimes graded to help people know how wild—or mild—they are. A grade one river is easy to ride. A grade six river is almost impossible to ride. However, rivers can change. Heavy rain can flood a river and can turn a grade one river into a dangerous river.

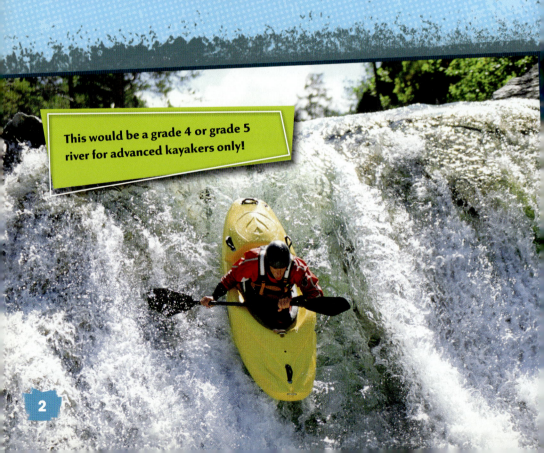

This would be a grade 4 or grade 5 river for advanced kayakers only!

This river has smaller waves.
It would be a grade 1 or grade 2.

HOW RIVERS ARE GRADED

Grade 1	• easy to ride • small waves and few obstacles • easy route to see
Grade 2	• reasonably hard to ride • minor obstacles, such as low drops and bends • medium–sized waves
Grade 3	• difficult to ride • small waterfalls and exposed rocks • large waves • have to follow a certain route
Grade 4	• very difficult to ride • whirlpools, drops, and exposed rocks • severe waves • route is not clear
Grade 5	• extremely difficult to ride • hidden hazards • powerful waves
Grade 6	• almost impossible to ride • severe risk to life

HOW KAYAKS ARE DESIGNED

River kayaks must be strong to survive a ride down the wild, white water. They are usually made of strong plastic or fiberglass. They are shorter than other kayaks, which helps them turn and twist quickly down the rapids.

River kayaks have a flat bottom. This design makes them easy to turn, but also easy to tip over.

The raised space at the front of a river kayak is for the kayaker's knees. A kayaker uses his or her knees to help turn the boat.

PARTS OF A KAYAK

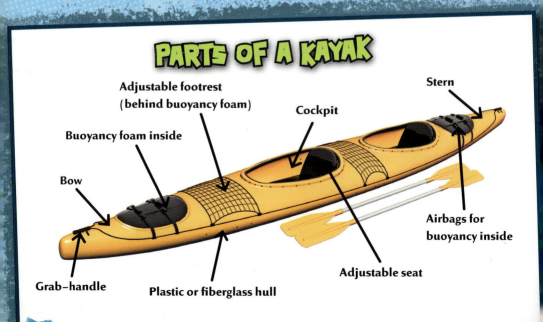

Adjustable footrest (behind buoyancy foam)

Cockpit

Stern

Buoyancy foam inside

Bow

Airbags for buoyancy inside

Grab–handle

Plastic or fiberglass hull

Adjustable seat

Kayaks and canoes look similar, but there is a difference. A paddle with two blades pushes a kayak along. A paddle with one blade pushes a canoe along.

River kayaks can reach top speed quickly.

A spray skirt is not essential, but it helps keep water out of the kayak. It fits around a person's waist like a skirt and fits over the rim of the cockpit.

WHY KAYAKERS USE SPECIAL GEAR

Kayaking down a river can be risky. There are many dangers, such as hidden rocks and fallen trees. One of the most important pieces of equipment for a kayaker is a helmet to protect the head from injuries. It should not be too loose or too tight.

A buoyancy vest is important, too. If a kayaker tips over in the water, it will help keep him or her afloat.

These kayakers have the right gear to go kayaking.

HOW TO LAUNCH A KAYAK

There are several ways to launch a kayak. For beginners, it is best to learn in calm, shallow water.

1. Place the kayak parallel to the riverbank.

2. Put the paddle across the kayak, behind the cockpit. One end of the paddle rests on the bank.

3. Grip the paddle to the edge of the cockpit. Slowly, put one foot into the kayak, follow with the other foot, and then sit down.

4. Use the paddle to push away from the bank.

It's important to sit up in your kayak instead of leaning back.

HOW TO PADDLE AND TURN

Once in the kayak, it is time to start paddling. A paddle for kayaking has a blade at each end. Pulling a blade through the water makes the kayak go forward. Pushing a blade through the water makes the kayak go backward.

When riding down a river, kayakers need to turn their boats. They do this by paddling on the side opposite of where they want to turn. To turn a kayak to the right, kayakers paddle on the left. To turn to the left, they paddle on the right.

If a kayaker keeps paddling on one side, they will go around in circles!

HOW TO REVERSE PADDLE

1.

Put the paddle parallel to the boat with the blade flat on the water.

2.

Push the blade down in the water and push forward with the bottom hand until the top hand is raised to about eye height.

3.

Finish the stroke as the blade leaves the water. Look behind you on the same side every second stroke to help guide your direction.

HOW TO GET OUT OF A KAYAK

Sometimes kayaks tip over with kayakers in them. It is important that the kayaker gets out of the boat—and fast! It is also important that they do not panic.

First, they must pull the tag on the spray skirt. Then they roll forward, with their head leaning toward the deck of the kayak. Sometimes they use their arms to push on the sides of the kayak. Once out of the boat, they use the grab–handle to tow it to shore.

Sometimes kayakers do not manage to grab their kayaks. They must avoid the hidden dangers under the water. They should float on their backs, with their feet up and their hands crossed over their chest.

This kayaker has tipped out of his boat.

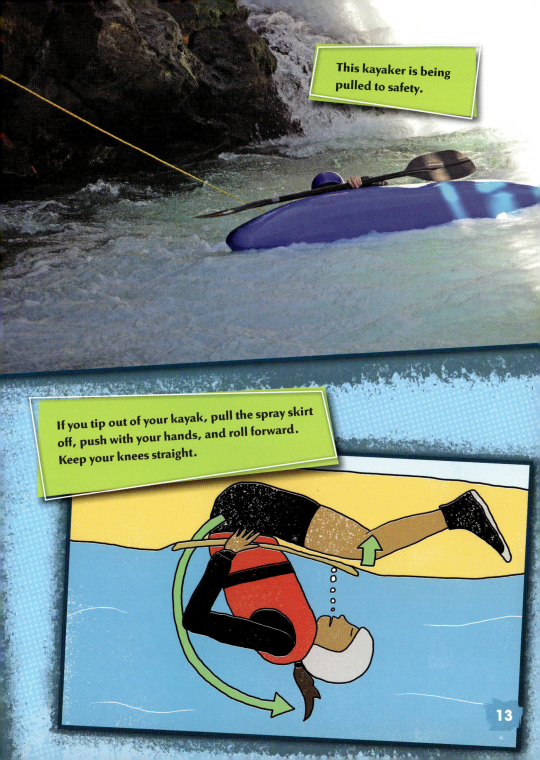

This kayaker is being pulled to safety.

If you tip out of your kayak, pull the spray skirt off, push with your hands, and roll forward. Keep your knees straight.

How to Roll a Kayak

Sometimes it is not safe for kayakers to leave their boats. Instead, they roll their boats back up using their legs, hips, and paddle.

Long ago, the Inuit peoples of North America used kayaks for hunting. They invented what people today call the Eskimo roll. The water was so cold in those parts that a hunter in an upturned kayak could freeze to death.

A kayaker shows how to do an Eskimo roll on the right side.

HOW TO DO AN ESKIMO ROLL

1. Hold the paddle parallel to the kayak on the left side.

2. Roll your wrists forward and sweep your body under the water.

3. Flick the hips quickly upward, toward the surface. At the same time, pull down with your right hand.

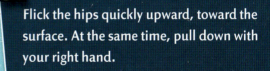

4. Twist to the back right corner of the kayak. The head is last to exit the water.

WHY KAYAKERS MUST READ A RIVER

To paddle safely down a river, kayakers need to be able to read a river. There are clues on the surface of a river to let them know what is happening under the water.

eddy

Rivers have calm water, too. These are called eddies. They are usually downstream of a headland or large rock.

A stopper or hole is a powerful wave that flows backward. It can stop or trap a kayak. These are very dangerous.

stopper

INDEX

INFORMATIONAL EXPLANATIONS

Explanations explain how things work and why things happen.

How to Write an Informational Explanation

STEP ONE

Select a topic.
Make a list of things you know about the topic.
Brainstorm the questions you need to ask.

Riding the River

How do people know about what rivers they can ride?
How are kayaks designed?
Why do kayakers use special gear?
How do people launch kayaks?
How do you paddle and turn kayaks?
How do you get out of a kayak that has tipped over?
How do kayakers "read" a river?

STEP TWO

Research the thing you need to know.
Use different resources for your research.

Internet, Library, Television Documentaries, Experts

Take notes or make copies of what you find.

STEP THREE

Sort through your notes. Organize related information under specific headings.

Why Kayakers Use Special Gear

Rivers can be dangerous
• rocks, fallen trees

Kayakers need
• helmets to protect their heads
• buoyancy vests to keep themselves afloat

STEP FOUR

Use your notes to write your Explanation.

• Introduce your topic.

• Add facts, details, and definitions from your research.

• Use quotations, examples, and vocabulary related to the topic.

• Use linking words and phrases, such as *another, for example, also,* and *because*.

• Provide a conclusion.

Your Explanation could have...

a table of contents

an index

Some explanations have a glossary.

Guide Notes

Title: Riding the River

Stage: Advanced Fluency

Text Form: Informational Explanation

Approach: Guided Reading

Processes: Supporting Comprehension, Exploring Language,
Processing Information

Writing Focus: Informational Explanation

SUPPORTING COMPREHENSION

- What do you think is the purpose of this book?
- How does the introduction text on page 2 explain the idea behind the topic?
- What inferences can you make about how people approach the process of grading a river?
- Why do you think it is important for a kayak to be turned or twisted quickly when riding rapids?
- What inferences can you make about the injuries that kayakers might face without their safety gear?
- Why do you think it is important for people to grip the paddle to the cockpit when getting into a kayak?
- How effectively has the author described the way to turn the boat? What helped you understand the information?
- What inferences can you make about what kayakers should do to enhance their safety when preparing to ride a river?
- How do you think kayakers should inspect their gear before going in the water?
- What questions do you have after reading the text?
- What helped you understand the information?

EXPLORING LANGUAGE

Vocabulary
Clarify: rapids, mild, plastic, fiberglass, buoyancy vest, parallel, cockpit, read a river
Synonyms: Discuss synonyms for *wild*, *mild*, *strong*, *dangers*
Antonyms: Discuss antonyms for *calm*, *opposite*, *important*

Print Conventions
Focus on punctuation: commas to make sense of complex sentences
Bullet points